EMERGENCE

Out of the Dawn

Kiki Yaw Sarpong

Dedication

To all the truth-tellers. May the truth always find a way.

Contents

August 15th, 2018

I don't remember exactly when I opened my eyes; I only remember when my consciousness finally interpreted the spinning blades dangling on my ceiling. They spun with resistance, the sound of an old motor working its tired limbs as it had for many a time. The blades pushed themselves as they had been instructed, compliant and without question of their master's order, swirling the air current to make my room feel cooler than it actually was.

The forced air pressed against my skin with a chill I adored, comforting me within the darkness of my four walls. I turned in delight to expose my other regions to experience the same comfort, and in that moment it felt like the best decision I had ever made.

My bed creaked in opposition to the movement, but I had no care for the complaints of the inanimate. I turned again, indecisive of the position to which I should return to slumber. The light from the alarm clock flashed in my eyes before I could close them again; amidst the darkness, its dim red light shone like the end of a tunnel. Its words, **"3:43 am"** signifying the dawn of the morning.

I smiled a wide crooked smile seeing the pleasant news that I had more hours of sleep till 7 am. I pushed my head deep into the softness of the pillow, letting my mind wander till sleep came for me again.

Sleep never came.

I turned around some more, a new position perhaps? Or maybe if I turned around enough, my body would finally take the hint and drift into nothingness.

It never did.

I opened my eyes again to the dark room and my pupils greeted it with familiarity. I could see the outlines of my surroundings frozen in place in this darkness, like a shaded charcoal painting, except for my ceiling fan; my industrious white fan that kept brightening the room with its flavor of chilled air.

I turned again in the direction of my night-stand and the time now read "**3:51 am**". Those past eight minutes were like thirty, and my frustration had started to simmer. I needed all the rest I could get after the turmoil of today. I had three news stories to finish before this weekend and none of them were even halfway done.

Not the story of the growing concern of the Asuma bridge; a bridge that was completed only three years ago now showing signs of rust and cracks on its underside. After weeks of tracking down one of the contractors and being so close to getting hard evidence of the misuse of funds along with the use of shoddy building materials, he disappeared into the wind without a trace, leaving me exactly where I started — with nothing.

I could have sufficed with my story on the country's minister of health laundering money through his various sham businesses. The revealing story of him siphoning dirty money into his account legally. However, my source has had the fear of God put in her and won't back me if I decide to go public. Again, leaving me with nothing but just my word, and a journalist's word without evidence means nothing, only speculation. I might as well be an internet blogger.

My last resort was to follow a story of a woman claiming ghosts had been stealing her chickens; my only story with a willing source who also claims to have irrefutable evidence. I'd have to travel three hours just to get to her location, and who knows how long I would have to stay just to complete the story.

Either-way, something has to pay the bills and fortunately for me, stories about spiritual thievery always seem to sell more newspapers. People will talk about it for days and the laughs will last for weeks. I can already see the mocking grin on my editor-in-chief's face, her roaring laughter already rippling in my ears.

"*This is definitely going on the front page,*" she would say through her laughter.

We both knew why it had to make the front cover even if deep down I hated the reason more than she did. We knew that people cared for the laughs more than the truth, or maybe the truth was always so depressing that they'd rather have some cheap laughs and go about their day than read another story of their leaders failing them again.

"*The truth hurts,*" is a saying we hear often but no one talks about what happens after the truth has hurt you too many times to count.

People become dulled to it, actively wish to escape it, or just ignore it altogether. Anything other than another story of an incompetent politician, a person hurting another for money, or a system that was made with the intention of benefiting everyone now only working to benefit a privileged few.

I remember the day I realized I was the bearer of bad news, two years after I had received my degree in journalism and working a career I had always dreamed of. I had just finished my story on a popular restaurant chain who were mixing the meat of different obscure animals and selling them in place of more sought-after meat. I presented my story with enthusiasm to my old editor-in-chief expecting praise, and he responded with a frustrated sigh.

"*Do you ever try to get any appealing stories? People don't like buying our newspaper because of these kinds of stories. They want to hear about gossip, celebrity news and some scandal. The Boatem restaurants are very popular for a reason; if people hated the meat, they won't keep going back to them. Our sales plummet every time we give your stories a big page. I know you invest a lot of time into these stories, but could you pivot to more entertainment-based stories?"*

I quit right there.

I had never done anything so sudden in my life. I have always been methodical and calculated in my actions, but in that moment, nothing felt better than leaving that job. Even with my awareness of my naivety in how the world perceived news stories, I have always been adamant about the type of work I wanted to do. I studied journalism because I always loved to find the truth, I loved to shine a light on falsehood and reveal what was true for everyone to see. I hated imposters and pretenders; I hated systems that sought to deceive and the people who worked alongside it.

When I was eight, I spent hours in the library to learn the secrets of a magic trick our teacher did just so I could show the entire class it was only sleight-of-hand trickery and not actual magic. When I was thirteen, I successfully caught and presented evidence to our school board that one of the upper-class students was taking bribes to change exam scores and give the more privileged students better scores because he had access to the headteacher's office.

Of course, they called me all sorts of names that lasted all through my high school but I never cared one bit. That senior was a menace who extorted most of the little my friends had, just so he'd acknowledge them, for he'd also lower scores if he disliked you. Nobody wanted to say a thing for fear of being ostracized, not believed, or suffering any other form of punishment. Everyone feared him, but not me, not Daniel Akwasi Aboagye. I outed him and all his lackeys, and I held my head high throughout my entire tenure in the school. I never stood for injustice — not now, not ever.

My path was carved for me before I even knew I had to take a path. My blood has always craved justice and my soul has yearned for factuality.

Though I must admit that as I have grown older, these terms don't seem as simple as I viewed them before. I used to believe all I had to do was present the truth and my job would be done, all would be right with the world and the imposters would disintegrate into dust.

How naive I was!

Now as I lay with the knowledge and wisdom of a twenty-nine-year-old man, I find that the truth is but a fraction of the complexity. Even armored with the strongest evidence, I rarely manage to make a chink in the defense of falsity. I fight misinformation, violence, threats, ignorance, unwillingness and surrender every day, and as strong as I think I am, I always find myself on the losing end.

I dove into journalism expecting glory and justice, for people to hail me as a "*truth-teller*" and acknowledge my efforts on discovery of truth. I wanted to be the catalyst for change, to improve the lives of the people around me while uplifting my community and country. I wanted my work to have meaning, not only for me, but also for those who couldn't request it for themselves. But here I lay, a couple of hours away from chasing stories about ghosts and chickens, working as a freelance journalist with little money to my name. I know this path was chosen for me; however, I always wonder if I made the right decision accepting it.

My parents would laugh if they ever heard me acknowledge that. They wanted me to be a lawyer or an engineer or some other dull high-profile job where I could make lots of money and have no impact. But I stood my ground against their united front and decided to work this low-profile job where I have no impact and get paid close to nothing — what a great idea.

I was young and inspired by truth and other famous journalists like Ola Benson, who broke the news on the government secretly stealing land and selling it off to foreign entities to build their secluded infrastructure.

Or Mathias Kofi Drew who exposed inhumane and racist conditions that foreign companies located in the country put local workers through. And not forgetting Antoinette Ababio, who unmasked the country-wide hack that disclosed the uber loss of medical, banking and social records of numerous citizens. I hoped to break the biggest stories that had people rushing to get a piece. I still do; I still dream of the chance. However, I'm old enough to know that dreams are only that — dreams.

Ding!

The light from my phone brightened up the room. My awareness flickered back into my eyes; realization dawned that I had been lying on my bed for longer than I thought. I had let my mind wander too far off and it had spun a wheel of my memories and desires, unperturbed. The giver of sleep had left me to my own whims and fantasies.

The sound of a rotating blade flooded my ears as my realization settled. I glanced at the ceiling with its tethered spinning servant, still as industrious as ever with a chill as pleasing as ever. I reached for my phone from atop the night-stand to see who was texting me at such an odd hour. The screen lit again and "*Editor Esi*" shone bright on the text label with a message that read:

"*Yooo Danny, get on twitter now!!! Something crazy is happening in Liberia!!!!*"

I swiped into my phone's home page and clicked the icon with the big blue bird, confused at what would be so interesting to warrant a text from Esi at this hour. I clicked the first video available and in seconds my eyes widened.

Ever Connected, Ever Disconnected

My eyes hurt. My eyes sting.

I feel the tiny explosions in them that make me blink continuously. The light feels blinding now; the morning light. I missed its slow transition from the dawn I could recall. I have stared at the brightness of my screen for minutes — no, hours. I had switched to the view on my laptop to see things better, succumbing myself to the fullness of its artificial rays.

My focus had been unshaken, and I failed to realize the world still moved without my attention. I had stared at tweets, blogs, videos, and pictures. Whatever could be seen on the internet, I saw it. I have a knack for searching for things in the right places.

My emotions hadn't settled regardless. I wasn't even sure what kind of emotions I was feeling at the moment if I were to be honest.

As part of the early witnesses to the anomaly, I was haunted by the mere extension of what was possible. The realization that what is unchangeable can now be changed. The mere idea breaks your mind, making you sit motionless at the edge of your bed at morning's light, staring into a screen with nothing but distraughtness.

I forgot to text Esi back. We had been on a call for over forty minutes before the network outage. A brief ten minutes of true disconnection from the world.

I jumped back into the chaos when the connections were restored. Network outages weren't uncommon, but in this situation, there was an extra layer of ominosity in the air. The discussions that existed were still as tumultuous as they had been at the beginning. People asking questions and only having answers filled with paranoia and full of conspiracy. I dabbled with similar results, though my questions plagued my mind in constant repetition.

How is it possible? Is it spreading? Will it happen to us too?

———

The first text I received from Esi, while bizarre, did nothing to prepare my expectations of what was new. I had opened the video with confusion, and I was met with even more.

They say it started around 3:17 am, or at least that's when people started to notice the influx of tweets and videos from the region. The late-sleepers from this time zone and the already-functioning from other time zones. It was a cry for help, a call for attention to the world amid desperation. The only problem was that the cry didn't make a lot of sense.

Initial speculation was that there was an earthquake happening in the Liberian city of Monrovia, however similar occurrences were reported in other Liberian cities like Buchanan, Tapeta, Ganta, Zwedru, and even in the bordering cities of Ivory Coast, Guinea and Sierra Leone. The messages poured in as a flood pours during a hurricane. The scale of this disaster was alarming.

I joined the audience at 3:52 am, immediately after the late-sleeper Esi reached out to me. She had been texting almost everyone from our office, though I was the only one still awake. When I finally witnessed the first-hand evidence of the event, it was a video of a family in Gbarnga, Liberia, recording the cracks that formed in the ground as entire buildings collapsed and the earth itself moved violently beneath their feet.

Their voices were loud, though still inaudible over the loud screams and the visible vapor that puffed from their mouths. They shivered, their dark skin transitioning to liquid blue as their feet lost their balance. The video swayed rampantly like a found-footage piece of cinema. The imagery was as helter-skelter as the people who filmed it, running in mindless directions to escape the inescapable.

The sounds were deafening. Prayers, calls for help, mindless screaming.

The darkness held them hostage with only hues of flashlights, phone screens and moonlight remaining. It was nothing short of horrific. My eyes gaped as did my mouth. I battled the authenticity of the imagery, checking for post dates and evidence of falsity.

In this age of misinformation, triple-checking sources was paramount.

"*This couldn't be true,*" was the only phrase I could summon in my mind. The next video changed my belief in an instant.

It was another video from the Liberian capital, showing the scale of destruction in the landscape. Buildings collapsed like a house of cards; the grounds moved as if something was coming from underneath it. Something blue and glistening, though still dark like the skies of a chilly fall evening.

The city lights here were still bright due to electricity, and the sounds from the video were clearer. The person filming was running through the chaos still swaying the camera around in anxiety, however his words were loud and clear. He repeated it over and over as he ran.

"*It is cold, it is so cold. The ground is breaking, the ground is changing.*"

I watched many videos since, too many to count. So much destruction in such a short span. I watched their dying messages populate the virtual presence of the internet, each new one overwriting the previous. They poured in so heavily and so suddenly, already the most trending topic in the world; then they stopped. Silent and dead.

It was estimated that the last upload from Liberia was around 4:22 am, because that's when people started to post about the radio silence from the country. People couldn't reach family, friends, workers, etc., anymore, not even ones who were actively on the phone with them just a few moments prior. The whole country was quiet.

Esi first called me around 4:31 am; her voice was trembling and held traces of someone who had been shedding tears. Her brother was married to a Liberian woman and unbeknownst to me, they had traveled to her home country to visit her family over a month ago. Both parents and their two children.

"*I can't reach my brother or his wife, I can't reach any of them.*"

"*They're saying it was a series of earthquakes all over the country. All a size ten on the Richter scale. How is that even possible? How is that ev...*"

Her voice trailed and I could hear her internal struggle to avoid breaking into tears. I comforted her the best way I could. Trying to encourage strength and hope even when I lacked those sentiments myself. I had known Esi for years; she was one of the strongest-willed people I had ever met and I failed her in this moment of vulnerability. For my emotions betrayed my words and she could feel my own lack of conviction.

Nevertheless, I pursued on, trying to find a sliver of hope to hold onto, hope that washed away as fast as I could conjure it.

The latest video posts that came in were perspectives from neighboring countries; Sierra Leone, Guinea, Côte d'Ivoire, and ones from satellite imagery. The Satellite imagery showed a complete darkness over the entire country with only little flickers of light at extreme ends of the southern border. The land was darker than usual.

The videos from neighboring countries were even more disturbing. They showed a different insight into the disaster. Is that even what this was? It didn't look like any kind of disaster we were familiar with.

I watched the videos with the same emotions as those who filmed it — horror.

I felt a chill run through my bones, the one that makes the hair on your skin stand upright and electrifies your senses. I'd been embraced by fear, and I hated its presence.

Still, my curiosity overpowered my need to look away. Could I even look away? I needed to know what caused this, not only to scratch the itch in my mind, but to recognize what might also be my destruction.

My country isn't far off from ground zero; how do I know that it won't spread here? At least I can face it with some semblance in my eyes if I ever had to.

Is it better to know the cause of your death than to not know?

I never thought about that. I never think about death because of superstition. Why plague your mind with thoughts of something you're actively trying to avoid. I was told at an early age that what you invite into your mind is what you invite into your life. I had grown enough to know that this wasn't always true, though I still lacked the courage to go against the grain. The only thought I had allowed about my death was to die at the age of ninety surrounded by my children and grandchildren.

Ninety feels like a good age to go, I'd hate to grow any older and lose my bodily autonomy. Needing people for everything sounds exhausting. I guess now my fantasy is in jeopardy.

"Eiiiiiiiishh ... *Danny, have you seen this? Oh God ... Oh God. What is happening!*"

Esi's voice re-emerged from the phone. She had muted herself for a while, shielding her tears from my ears, and I gave her the space to grieve. My phone lit up for a second and I opened the link she provided. It was a video from Côte d'Ivoire, another video showing more insight on the disaster.

I hated that she saw it, a sad hate of what it meant for her. The finality of what the video dictated was something that depleted all hope.

The video was from a village in the more rural extremes of Ivory Coast, one that was close to the south-western border of the country. It showed the destruction in the land that extended into the country of ivory, and the scale was unimaginable.

The annihilation had traveled just enough to reach their doorstep, like an unwelcome guest staring into their souls with intimidation.

For some reason, the destruction had stopped just a few feet from them, giving them a first-person view of the new-world disaster. A demolition that had finally drawn a battle line in the sand.

The light of dawn in the video marked its recency, brightening it for all to see as clearly as possible.

The terrain from the area of the disaster had sort of tilted, filled with large cracks and spikes from the ground. Land cracked as wide as the length of long buses, separating what was once together into asunder. It was as if the land had been hit with a large hammer, deforming it into broken shapes and jagged edges.

The once flat plain was unrecognizable from what it once was. The dust that covered it seemed dense and full of menace, though the most alarming thing of all was the glistening blue coils that emerged from the ground. They looked like the roots of an unbelievably large tree, diving into the ground and reappearing like dolphins do when swimming, extending their reach over the large terrain. They leached and coiled into the lands, long and large, pulsing like a live being sucking the life out of the earth. Everything behind them was left in black and darkness.

The trees in the rear were withered and shrill, the land had lost its brown coloration, and it was evident that there was no life behind them. The blue coils sprouted as many as the dark vines of a dark forest, and there was no doubt that they had claimed everything as their domain.

The locals in the video wore their emotions in their voices; fear, curiosity, confusion. They gathered close, some inching closer to the line drawn in the sand.

The person filming spoke clearly, but I couldn't decipher his words. I knew only a little French from my high school days, at least the ones I retained, though I was sure that he spoke a different local dialect. He turned the camera to face himself and spoke some more before turning it back. A mixture of fear and curiosity painted his youthful expression. He panned the camera around to show the scale of the destruction while the crowd continued their deliberation, some moving away and others moving toward it.

A tall lanky man was the first to cross the border. Why anyone would do that, I have no idea. As humans our first instinct is to move from perceived danger; even animals are evolved enough to also exhibit this instinct. Why anyone would willingly move toward the unknown I cannot understand, but this man still moved. His reasoning will be only known to him and his god.

He walked with a bold curiosity, stepping over the darkened ground till he reached one of the blue vines. The voices of the crowd had mostly subsided into murmurs except for a few who barked orders at him, whether in approval or disapproval, I wish I knew. Regardless, he reached toward a piece of the vine, and the moment he touched it, it sprouted and absorbed him, extending more toward the crowd.

The video stopped there.

The last sound being the sudden uproar of dread, and the last blurry frame showing the speed at which they ran.

More videos followed from different regions experiencing similar predicaments; it didn't take long for people to realize the vines were hostile and dangerous. The world watched as well, everyone who knew about the anomaly now sharing the same fear, curiosity and confusion at varying levels.

Esi had muted me again. I felt the silence once the video stopped. I couldn't imagine how hard this was for her. What was the right thing to say at this moment? I wish I knew. All the words I could think of sounded incomplete in my mind. Maybe it's better to say nothing and just be on the phone with her, or maybe that was my coward's way out.

I finally mustered the courage to say something of solace, some generic speech I could conjure to console my friend's grieving heart. I grabbed my phone to speak, and my phone screen interrupted me with a giant "Call Failed" sign. As if it was mocking my intentions.

I tried to call her again before noticing my network had disappeared.

Damn this network company!

This wasn't the time for their low-grade service to impact an important moment. How easy it was for them to cut me off from the rest of the world. A forced ejection from the global highway of communication.

I sat there quietly, staring at both screens, my eyes still hypnotized by their light.

I sat there quietly, my emotions rumbling in a whirlwind and my mind silenced.

I sat there quietly, connected to the world, yet disconnected from it.

What Did the World Say?

The sun bid farewell in a glorious exit. Frankly, not any different than it always was.

I stood outside Kuffour Street, a few blocks from my residence, staring into the golden skies and layered clouds. A mix of warm yellow and soft orange splashed into the horizon beyond, painting the skies in the west a farewell portrait. The once scattered clouds had now clustered together as if to create a stairway into heaven. I stared at this scene and felt nothing inside. Not a single sense of admiration filled my heart, and my senses didn't spark to its magnificence.

Am I numb to beauty?

What I could feel were its last warm rays kissing my skin as gently as a mother would kiss her baby. My skin soaked in the vitamins with gratitude.

I continued to stare into the skies contemplating my lack of appreciation. Had I seen too many sunsets to lose respect for its glory? Maybe if I saw it from atop a mountain, or the edge of a high-rise building, it would feel different. Seeing it through the occlusion of scattered two-story buildings and small urban houses didn't prompt the same emotion. I guess it would be right for me to also acknowledge that I might have used up all my emotions for the day. My mind and soul had been heightened with feelings since dawn, and my body was all out of any emotions.

I broke from my stare into the horizon and started my journey back home.

I had called my family as early as I knew they would be up. The bearer of bad news strikes again, here to inform everyone of the disaster. I had no other input than to tell them to stay safe and stay informed. I'm not even sure what staying safe meant if the disaster hit us. Where could we even go? I doubt we could escape it. I could already feel my mother in deep prayer. She was a very religious woman, and even though I never picked up the habit, I know her prayers stood strong for us all. If there was a time to pray, this would be it.

I also called Esi back earlier in the morning to check in on her. The call failed the first two times before I got her on the third call. I assumed she would be home resting or even with her family, but no, she was at the office writing articles to update our news website and prepare for the next day's newspaper. I imagined she would have tried to update today's newspapers if she could, but the papers were already printed by midnight and scheduled to be distributed in the early morning, so that was set in stone.

I tried to convince her to take the day off as I had, but she wouldn't hear any of my pleas.

I had shelved my ghosts-and-chickens story thinking no one would care about that in such an unprecedented time; my mind had been racing only with thoughts about the things that happened this morning.

I had spent hours in front of screens, jumping from one screen to the other. The latest being my television.

Hearing and seeing on a bigger scale most of what I had already heard and seen. It still felt unbelievable even as the news anchors spoke the words and tried their best to maintain cheerful faces. I had wished this was one of the bad dreams I get to escape when I finally opened my eyes, but it wasn't. This was as real as the air I felt I was drowning in.

At 7 am, word had started to officially spread in the country. Every television and radio station had some aspect of it running. At 8 am, the national emergency alert system had been activated to inform everyone of the situation. As we were one of the closest countries to the disaster, tensions had risen quickly.

News from the countries that had experienced a first-hand interaction with the disaster stated that there had been no changes in the growth of the anomaly, and that locals had been advised to move further inland to escape any unpredicted growth — an advice that fell on deaf ears.

News poured in from many sources. Indeed, news travels fast, though acceptance of what is heard travels at one-tenth the same speed. I don't know what I expected the reactions to be, but it certainly wasn't what I imagined. Most people I met in the streets showed no signs of care or interest, a similar predicament that I had observed online outside of hyper-focused spaces I had been in.

I ignorantly assumed there would be wide interest when I finally stepped out of my apartment, but there was nothing. Actually, there was more than nothing, there was nonchalance.

Was it naive of me to think that people would care? Was it because they hadn't seen the many videos and tweets like I had? They hadn't been overwhelmed with the knowledge that there existed something that could annihilate them in mere moments. Why wouldn't they care? I assumed there would be more interest in the situation. Was that wrong of me? I sought to ask a couple of people I met outside on their thoughts of the situation, and their answers perplexed me even more.

"I don't think it's real. It feels like a hoax. The videos look edited to inspire chaos. This political party in power has always been deceitful."

"Yeah, I heard of it. I don't think it matters much since it's all the way in Liberia. How will it get here? I don't think we need to worry about it."

"I don't bother myself with all that, there's always some new disaster happening somewhere these days. I have a family of six to worry about."

"Oh that? I thought it was like a nationwide prank or something. Well, if it's real, what can I do about it? If it happens, it happens. I'm tired of living anyway."

Their indifference was a sentiment that others shared online too.

Once I stepped out of the virtual bubble of those who showed keen interest, into the shared highway of online public opinion, I realized that we had truly drifted away from being creatures of community. We all saw the same event but jumped to completely different conclusions. We had slowly developed group-individuality, where we cared only for small sections of things that only directly affected us.

An attachment to the word "my". Myself, my family, my city, my country.

We had forgotten that because we shared the same planet, we would always be indirectly connected, and hence always at risk of feeling the reverberation of things that happened far beyond our scope.

I'm not sure when this group-individuality fully formed; I reckon it was before I was born.

Or have we always been this way? Is this how we were always meant to be? I wish I could find the answer to that.

Regardless, I still scrolled through the online discourse. The ones speaking of dropping nuclear weapons on the Liberian country to make quick work of the threat. An easy solution to those who never had to experience the after-effects of their decisions.

The next were the growing opinions of the segregationists, those who were intensely advocating for quarantining the entire African continent. Spreading misinformation of the growth of a deadly virus on the continent, and the need to cut off the world from it before the people of Africa started to travel outside to other continents and affect them.

This opinion took a stronger hold than I imagined. I figured it was the many gruesome videos that spiked fear in people's hearts, though other emotions could have been at play.

I would admit that I didn't sit idly by while these asinine thoughts were being flaunted; I responded to many, as fruitless as that may seem. Commenting, posting, replying to people who never gave a second thought to their foolish opinions. I won't ask if they cared, cos I know they did not. Anybody willing to drop nuclear bombs on an entire country or forcefully segregate an entire continent for the greater good has lost a side of themselves they don't even realize. It was unfortunate, but I had no sympathy for their lost souls.

The many opinions still continued, with diverging views all worse than the next. The little crowds that cared were drowned in the giant chasm of chaos that floated above. As if they sank due to their profound density, sinking lower and lower as the views from the lighter-headed floated higher up the heap.

The sheer quantity was immense. Having the entire world converge on a singular topic was a recipe for calamity.

Another section of growing alarm was the conspiracy theories that formed. Conspiracies rooted in alien mythology, spiritual endeavors, religion, science, pseudo-science, and even into Greek mythology. One group claimed Liberia was the new Sodom and Gomorrah being cleansed for their sins; another claimed they had upset the native spirits and this was their judgment, while others mentioned that the country had discovered alien life and the aliens had taken over.

Surprisingly, all of them seemed to point to the end of the world being imminent. Their speculations rose and fell as mountains to valleys, corrupting the spread of news and expanding the flow of misinformation.

When the mental exhaustion of my exposure to these views started to flare, I retreated back into the virtual bubble that shared my interest and care for the event. I blocked out the noise and focused on what was important.

What caused this anomaly? Why now? What was it?

I've always believed in the law of cause and effect. Nothing truly happens out of the blue, especially not something as grave as this. The gears in my mind accelerated their spinning. What could I find about the cause; surely somebody knew something. Were they even alive or did they perish in the destruction?

Hmm. I couldn't rely on human sources this time. For this, I'd have to dig deep, deep into the singular global archive that held all our histories. The one where every-one willfully posted their worst and best moments, their unwarranted opinions, their desires and their thoughts. I would dig as much as I could, till I found something that would lead me in the direction of the truth. Till I found the light that would drive away all these falsities. That would be my purpose.

My legs broke from walking, and my subconsciousness returned command to my consciousness. My body had been on autopilot throughout my return, and the sight of the shiny brown gate of my building triggered the release to manual control. I took a look at my phone for the time, and "**6:49 pm**" stared back at me from the phone screen.

My stomach rumbled slightly seconds later, signaling me that the food I held in the plastic bag was getting cold. On cue, I smelled the sweet aroma of the Jollof rice, the soft fried plantains and roasted chicken thighs that awaited my consumption. My lips broke into a smile. There was much to do. The path before me was set, and I was ready for its trials.

I took another deep breath of appreciation before pushing the large brown gate open.

Matryoshka

I heard their voices again, plain and high-pitched.

Followed by thunderous steps slapping the ground with an intensity that made me share equal annoyance and admiration at how beings so small could make such loud noises. The heavy sounds died down for an unusual amount of time. Have they decided to rest now? Perhaps their small skinny legs had started to feel the recoil from their actions.

I doubted it.

My senses still stayed alert, keenly awaiting the moment the seismic shifting of earth's plates would start again. Who knew children could be so energetic? And six of them? I'm not sure when they collectively decided that the area outside my apartment would be their main playground.

I can't even remember the day it started; somewhere last month maybe. At first it was infrequent; then before I knew it, it was every other day. I had hesitated from speaking to avoid becoming the stereotyped "*get off my lawn*" old man, not that I was old. Unfortunately for me, my reluctance had been taken as acceptance of the new norm. Silence is indeed acquiescence. I had traded my peace in exchange for the title of a chill uncle, and I was reaping the benefits in the currency of irritating sounds.

I huffed inward. I'm not one to interrupt little children in the joys of their young pleasures, but I had had enough. The next time I heard any noise, I would storm outside with a belt in-hand.

My conviction strengthened.

Another sound jolted in, and I clenched my fist — it was neither that of the children or heavy steps. I turned to look at the notification that popped on my laptop and scooted my chair a bit closer to my work desk.

It was an update from CNN on the current situation of the disaster in Liberia. I opened the article and read through it as quickly as I could, then sighed. No new relevant news, just more generic speculations with no basis.

It was just a bunch of professional gibberish. What kind of journalists were they hiring? I could do a much better job than this.

Three days post the calamity that shocked the entire world, we were now in the early days of the aftermath. The mayhem after the storm. I had notifications for all relevant news websites, and all of them had nothing. Everyone was either reporting about some country sending a team to investigate the situation, or some other country exhibiting signs of paranoia and debating closing their borders.

Everyone was on edge.

The speculations were rampant; the controversies and conspiracies began to nest like Russian dolls, and soon opinions ranged to be more nonsensical than sensical. It kind of made sense in a weird way because what we knew about the world had been flipped on its head.

I had been on my own personal journey to find the truth, a journey that was also amounting to nothing.

For three days, I had combed through numerous videos searching for anything significant but to no avail.

There had been some updated satellite imagery of the destroyed country, a higher-quality look at the force of nature that had unraveled an entire nation. It covered the ground like a stain on the earth, absorbing the land but never the sea. Was it against water? It seemed to have no issue with the lakes and rivers it destroyed.

At this moment on the third day, I could feel the shame that crept up from my failures. I had jumped into my research full of energy and motivation, filled with delusions of grandeur, expecting the truth to call to me like the soft hymns of a charismatic church. But alas, I sit here with an empty notebook and barren ideas.

So much time wasted; I missed all of my deadlines for my actual work, the ones I get paid for, the ones that pay the bills. Freelance work means I get to work at my own time, though without results, my coffers would stay empty. I needed to reach out to Esi to seek an extension. I should have done that two days ago, I just couldn't find the courage to type the words out.

I felt my reasoning was inferior, I still feel like it is.

I snapped out of my emotions back to the glare of the screen that stared back at me. I had been scrolling social media for days. Facebook, Twitter, Instagram, Reddit, Discord, back to Facebook. Wherever I felt like I could search for an ounce of legitimacy in information.

It was harder now because of the influx of information; more opinions meant more garbage, and it was harder to filter through the cesspool.

Censoring had also started to become an issue, videos were being removed at a fast pace, and I had to search fast before I lost vital information. Where to search was the problem. I had filters for location and date, though that didn't seem to be enough. Sorting the Liberian videos didn't seem to be of any use when all the videos were uploaded around the same time.

I opened twitter back again, back to my scheduled viewing of the horrific videos. Being exposed to people's last moments over and over again.

One after the other I watched, looking at multiple perspectives of the same thing and concluding with no additional information.

I had developed a routine. I would watch a video and analyze it the best I could for any new information, then click on the person's profile and say a prayer of farewell. It seemed like the right thing to do for people who most likely had no more families to mourn them. People who had been lost to the essence of history.

I clicked on the next video and it was of an older man, his profile picture still bright with a colorful smile. I skimmed through his profile to get to know him, the digitized version of him that was portrayed to the world.

He was a pharmacist living in Buchanan, Liberia; he had three daughters, one had just recently gotten married. There was clearly a mother in the wedding pictures, but they didn't seem to have any pictures together or show any outward affection toward each other. I safely assumed they were divorced when I noticed the absence of a ring on his finger. He had no grandchildren but had immense affection for his cat who he posted frequently. A white and ginger-haired Norwegian-forest cat.

I smiled at their bond and closed my eyes, parting my lips to pray that they were in a better place before moving on to the next video.

The next video was short, about forty-five seconds of mostly quick sways and incoherent sounds. I thought to skip it for a moment before relenting on that idea. I clicked the profile to see its owner; a teenage girl about the age of fifteen to seventeen wearing a pair of edgy dark shades in her profile picture. A teenager trying her most to look cool.

Her account was small, less than sixty followers, and she had just joined the platform a little over a year ago. She had a lot more videos however, mostly of her small town and some lifestyle videos with her friends. She posted a lot, not that surprising for a teenager. Her location on her profile was Dawota, a small rural town in the heart of Liberia, but she frequented a bigger town named Gbarnga very often. I checked the distance, and Dawota was just about eight kilometers from Gbarnga.

Her visits to the town had a different version of her compared to the versions of videos from Dawota. In Gbarnga, she was dressed differently. More revealing clothes and an aggressive touch of makeup. She was in a nicer car, visited fancier restaurants and hotels. It was clearly a case of a teenager living a double life.

My natural curiosity got the better of me and I tried to find out who this sponsor for her separate lifestyle was, but she rarely filmed the person. I assumed it was only one.

I dug deeper into her media till I was as far in as the beginning of her account, and there he was, three-quarters of his face showing in a slightly distorted mirror reflection from a video she took inside a house.

He was a middle-aged Caucasian man who looked to be in his late fifties or early sixties. From her content, he seemed to be a teacher from the number of books, papers, and material he kept. Even though she never showed the man in most of her videos, his stuff was always littered around somewhere in her videos.

I checked under the video-post and there was one comment under it; it was from another teenage girl. I opened her account, another small account and recognized her from the previous girl's lifestyle videos. She was one of her friends from Dawota.

This second girl had no videos of the disaster. In fact, she hadn't even posted for about two weeks. I searched her media and to my surprise, her media was awfully similar to the first girl's content. This girl was also living a double life.

There was a difference however with this girl, she had no issue showing the man she was with. They had many videos and pictures together like actual couples do.

It was another middle-aged Caucasian man, a bit younger than the previous. She mentioned his name in one of the videos — Mathéo. He also seemed to be a teacher, a math teacher probably, based on written math equations that were common in papers and books that showed in the background of her video content. She didn't have a lot of videos compared to the first girl, but hers had more quality to them. There was always something new to decipher from it. She had little restrictions in what she posted to the world; I doubt she cared.

I also doubt he was aware she was posting these videos, or maybe he was and also didn't care.

She had videos showing the gifts he bought for her; jewelry, mobile devices, books. Then videos of him sleeping, videos of her talking about her love for him, videos of her cooking for him, and more. Her life seemed to revolve around him. She spoke about him with a joy that saddened me. Did her parents even know about this? Or they did and condoned it?

I opened another video of her unboxing a gift.

"Ooohh guys see ... see what my science-man got me ..."

The name triggered me, this wasn't the first time she called him that. It was like a pet name she referred to him by, many times in other videos. Was he a math and science teacher? Were both of these men foreign educators who were taking advantage of these gullible teenagers instead of impacting a meaningful education? I guess it wouldn't matter now that they were all dead. I should leave this matter alone and continue on the path I originally decided on.

Well ... if only I could find the NGO they worked under, I was certain there was a non-governmental organization responsible for pushing these predators into these areas.

I would give myself just a little time to figure it out, and if I couldn't, I would leave it alone and continue on my main journey, the one that was most important.

They say a picture is worth a thousand words, so what then is the worth of a video? I had paid too much attention to the foreground and not enough to what lay underneath.

I was curious about the equations. My initial assumption was just generic math as any normal person does when they see anything math related. I was never good at math and did my very best to avoid it in all situations.

Taking a second look at some of the writings I saw after zooming in-depth into the video, these equations weren't some of the simple ones I was used to. They looked more complex than high school or college-level math. I picked up a pen and wrote some of the shorter ones down and googled some of them.

Some generated results and others didn't. The results were a mixture of biological and chemistry equations.

The Nernst equation, the Henderson-Hasselbalch equation, the Michaelis–Menten enzyme kinetics equation.

These didn't sound like anything a normal teacher would be actively working with. It could be debated that this was an advanced level college class, though I doubted the closest universities in the area offered any of these courses.

I continued to look for more clues in the videos. I began to notice a trend in the attire the man wore. There was always something around with the "University of Cambridge" text on it. Some kind of apparel, a book, shirt, bag, or hat. It was clear that this man had a fascination with this university, a fascination that people who attended the school would have. Though if he attended it, I would assume that was long ago. I would have to look too far deep to even confirm that he was a student. How would that even help me? It would reduce my region of search, I guess.

I opened google again and typed in "*Mathéo university of Cambridge*".

The text output was long and full of garbage so I switched to the images tab and scrolled through it. This output wasn't as long. I scanned through the individual photos and found no resemblance. There were a few group photos however, and on the third group picture all the way in the left corner of the screen, I saw him. In an image dated about four years ago titled, "*Meet the pioneers behind the great breakthrough in science.*"

An article linking to a scientific paper about advancements in synthetic biology and micro-organism engineering, with a group picture of eight scientists attached to it.

There he was, all the way to the right of the picture, Dr. Mathéo Laurent with a title of professor in molecular biology at the University of Cambridge, and ... wait is that......? I know that face.

Yes, the other guy from before. That is him.

Dr. Henri Dupont, professor of biochemistry and cell biology at Université Paris Cité.

What is going on here? How are these two men anywhere near Dawota, Liberia? Was it for research or for their despicable pleasures?

They seemed to be still working while being there. What was I missing?

I glanced at the image with heavy confusion. What is going on here? I have been an investigative journalist all my life and my senses tend to spark when I sense a falsity in something, and for this, they were fully raging.

Conspiracy

I sat there quietly. My surroundings now more silent than they were about six hours ago, though the cacophony in my brain was blaring. The neurons in my head fired as fast as light fills a dark room. My thoughts considered possibilities upon possibilities, no single thought truly taking hold of my internal calamity and restoring order to the anarchy.

I sat there still.

The time was 9:39 pm. I discovered the names of the two scientists about six hours ago; that was when my analysis really began. In about two hours, I had found everything about them, everything that was open to the public that is.

Mathéo was the easiest to find. An award-winning molecular biologist with multiple books and papers on the subject. He had a very active social media presence on Facebook until two years ago, that's when his posts slowed, and he began to post about once every quarter on average. He was a professor at the university of Cambridge from 2010 to 2016. He was listed to be a French national in most of the sources I visited. He had lecture videos about many complex concepts of biology that went over my head when I watched them. He had no wife and no kids, and most of his family were never listed anywhere except for a brother — Louis Laurent, a dentist in Lyon, France.

Mathéo appeared in many other areas, all seeming to stagnate around the years 2015 to 2016.

I also found nothing linking him to his location in Liberia. The more I looked into him, the more he seemed out of place in Gbarnga.

Dr. Henri Dupont was harder to find. His name was a common French name which unfortunately always leads to harder searches. I went through multiple pieces of media to no results. The existing picture of him with the eight scientists was the only source I could follow.

I cropped out his picture from the larger image and ran google image searches on it plus his name but got nothing significant, only some sketchy website full of French words and military jargons. I translated the text to English and it read as some ambiguous text on military personnel. Nothing relevant to my search.

The Université Paris Cité also didn't have any public data on him. He wasn't listed as part of their current professors, and all of his papers were behind a paywall.

I switched my focus to searching in his field. If I could look for top-level scientists who worked on similar things in his region, perhaps I could find him too.

This approach was time consuming, but after an hour I found him through the help of Dr. Anne Koslov, a chemistry professor at Sorbonne Université. In an Instagram post she made in 2013, *"Enjoying a Merry Christmas with my favorite colleagues."*

He stood there in full revelation. There was even a video attached in the post, and the best thing of all was he had an Instagram account that commented on it.

Bingo!

I opened the account and his life opened to me.

He was a family man; his wife was a pale, tall blonde woman with freckles above her right eye. He had two sons and a daughter, and his latest post was for the birthday of his youngest son in May. I cross checked the date of the post with the account of the first girl from Dawota; he was with her the week prior.

I dove deep into his life, the one shown through the only social media account I could find. The pictures were mostly family pictures, his work in biochemistry, and a picture of some medals with the comment, "*Proud to be bestowed the utmost honor.*"

I took a picture of the bronze medal and searched for what it was.

The National Defense Medal; a military decoration awarded for exemplary military service.

He was a military scientist?

I paused to regain my thoughts when I saw the revelation. Everything about this seemed to get crazier the more I looked into the lives of these two people.

What was so special about that region in Liberia? There had to be something hidden that I was missing, or was I pulling on the wrong thread?

I suppose this could just be a story of two sinister men who traveled to this region to entertain their depraved fetishes, though I couldn't fully believe that myself. The puzzle for that analysis didn't seem to fit. Also why do I think it's just two? There could be more. Were they all scientists too?

Either way, I had to know definitively that there was no correlation here before I stopped pursuing this story. I can also admit that my reluctance to leave was because I had nothing going for the main story, and this advancement was the only intriguing hunch I had found in three days.

With that reasoning, I directed my focus to the region of Gbarnga for the last three hours, focusing on a fifteen-kilometer radius of the city.

I filtered everything else out, and this decision is the reason I sit here quietly at 9:39 pm with my mind blown.

The pieces fit ... they do.

I could feel the connection of the puzzles as they came together in coherence. There was a much larger story here, something dark, something inconceivable. I stared back in the direction of my watch as it turned 9:40 pm.

I could hear my loud exhale disturb my silence.

My attention moved to my fingers. I could feel the tiredness in my nerves, my dark knuckles absorbed the soft light from the fluorescent bulb and my skin looked weary. I knew I was tired. My spine complained from being glued to a chair for hours, my stomach nagged at me from hunger and my eyes ... my eyes felt no pain. Had they finally grown numb?

My mind contemplated my findings and still argued its validity amidst my conviction. My gut feeling and my final conclusion were at odds.

I can agree that my conclusion may sound strange at first, but my evidence tells a believable story ... it has to. Or have I finally turned into one of those absurd conspiracy theorists I despise so much? I reckon they also believe they are telling a believable story. Maybe I have spent too much time on this story and I'm drawing conclusions that don't exist?

No matter, I can't falter now. My gut tells me this is the way, and I trust my intuition. It has never led me astray.

This isn't a wild goose chase, there is truth to this story.

Still, my mind juggled different thoughts. I had to tell someone, someone I trusted, someone who knew what was at stake, someone analytical who wouldn't feed into my transgressions and would clearly tell me if I was wrong.

I picked up the phone and made the call; it rang for a while and then I heard her voice.

"Hey Danny, what's up?"

The Sins of a Monster

The knock on the door came at 10:12 pm, I muted my television and paced quickly to the door. I had turned on the television to get my mind off its hamster-wheel. To watch some random show while I waited, however I couldn't focus for long and very soon I was back watching CNN again.

I opened the door to reveal the one at its threshold.

"*You got here fast,*" was the first sentence to come from my mouth.

Esi entered the living room and took off her shoes by the door.

"Well, you sounded very cryptic, I dropped everything to come. What's going on?"

Her voice showed her concern, and her face couldn't hide the fact that she had been grieving her dead brother and his family for days. The bags under her eyes had aged her ten years; her hair was tied into a bun but you could tell she hadn't combed it in days. She wore a baggy red shirt and blue jean trousers, and she towered above me like she always did, tall and plus-sized.

"Oh Esi, your eyes ..." I couldn't finish my sentence but she knew what I meant.

I should have gone to see her days ago. I called her two days ago to check up on her and she told me she was fine and that I shouldn't visit. She told me she was with some family, and they were dealing with the loss together.

Should I have still gone to see her anyway? I probably should have.

And now I call her here for this. What type of friend am I?

I was worried about calling her for a work extension which ultimately didn't matter. I considered how personal this story would be to her, but did I not consider it enough?

"It's fine ... it's fine. My face gets like that sometimes. You called me here for something, what is it?" She retorted in response to my concern.

"C'mon Danny, I drove here for this."

I hesitated for a second before speaking. I motioned for her to take a seat on the couch and cleared the table from the leftover food I was eating before she arrived.

I grabbed my laptop and set it in front of her before beginning. I started with the first half of the story, my initial search of the cause of the anomaly and the futility in that endeavor. I talked about my continuing search till I encountered the two girls from Dawota and their double lives, the one that led to the discovery of the scientists. I spoke about the strangeness of the situation with the scientists and how something felt off about them.

I paused to see her reaction.

"Don't you find that strange?" I asked.

She looked at me thoughtfully and responded,

"Well, not too strange. Even if they aren't part of an NGO or some outreach organization, I understand it's uncommon to find two foreign molecular biologists in such

a remote city as Gbarnga. They were obviously there for their gross escapades. They could have always claimed they were there for some obscure research. And you can confirm they were frequenting the region for about two years? If so, that's eyebrow raising but I don't see how it still connects to what happened."

"So, what if I told you there were about fifteen scientists then." I countered.

I could see her eyes widen, same way mine did when I found out.

"Fifteen? All molecular French scientists?" She asked.

"Yes fifteen, all French scientists but not all molecular. And all very distinguished scientists in some field relating to cellular biology, genetics, energy and botany." I responded.

Her expression changed. The fold on her left eyebrow started to pop.

I knew that sign, I loved that sign.

It was one she had every time I was laying down a story she found interesting. I soaked in the positive reinforcement and continued.

The approximate three hours I had from 6pm to late around 9pm led me down a rabbit hole that connected threads upon threads till I found a giant well of evidence. I had information on the first two scientists but nothing good, though that changed when I reduced my searching range to fifteen kilometers around Gbarnga. Very soon, that changed to six kilometers, and then to only Gbarnga and a new town named Gbilepa.

History was my friend, and every search opened something more till I was able to isolate these two places. My first meaningful piece of information was from a boy named Karim Buntu, a football player from a school in Gbarnga. Karim was interesting, but what was more interesting was who he led me to — his father Mohammed Buntu — a Liberian army officer stationed in Gbilepa.

Mohammed was another avid poster on social media. His preference being Facebook. Mohammed posted a lot, and even that was an understatement.

He was posted to a small military base in Gbilepa, an old base that is barely registered in any public Liberian databases, and described as inactive in the public databases I found. Mohammed's videos from the base painted an entirely different picture. Some of his latest videos showed significant advancement in the base, not in the structures, but the technology being used.

Anyone who knows a thing or two about most African military bases would be bewildered at the sight of this. They had large solar farms with giant panels to harvest energy; there were many mysterious pieces of equipment housed in multiple structures connected by large cable wires. The place was active with heavy trucks and forklifts moving equipment, and the most surprising thing of all was that for an African military base, the personnel didn't look the part. Some of the soldiers were clearly Liberian, but the base wasn't just full of soldiers.

From his videos I counted about thirty Liberian soldiers, ten additional Liberian personnel, twenty French personnel in tactical gear, eight French personnel in non-tactical gear, and fifteen French scientists.

The base was heavily fortified with automated machine weapons by the walls, and all the soldiers were heavily armed.

For such a secured base, I was surprised by how much this man got away with recording so much. He was a lower-level soldier who was mostly posted by the outside gate along with some of the other Liberian officers, and his colleagues themselves didn't mind the action. His videos of the place also showed that he had been there for only six months.

My curiosity for this particular location intensified. I had been able to confirm that the two scientists worked there when I saw Mathéo in the background of one of his videos. I hadn't seen Henri in them yet, but the soldier had a lot of videos, and I knew I would find him eventually in one.

I opened google-earth for satellite imagery, and scrolled back in time to view any changes in that particular location since 2015, an action which confirmed my hunch. There was little activity in the year of 2015, and even to the early weeks of 2016, but in April of 2016 there was a sudden spike in activity. New structures began to form after that month and that's when the progression started. The same time that coincided with Mathéo's disappearance from social media.

I searched for any noteworthy thing that happened in Liberia during this time, focusing on any mention of France, Gbarnga, military or Gbilepa. The only results I got were the numerous articles of French aid to Liberia during the month of March 2016. The articles highlighted debt payoffs for the country, aid for education and health as well as military aid. It was an influx of goodwill from the foreign country in exchange for what?

I switched my search from March of 2016 to August 2016 leaving the same filters on. The results were articles for newspaper agencies and social media accounts that were mainly located in Gbarnga speaking to a "land reclamation" phenomena that was going on from the government. Certain pieces of land were being reclaimed and given to the "Abajou" — "the foreigners".

The content continues with videos and pictures that show the native people's reaction to seeing foreigners regularly, as well as the known location they resided at.

The locals had many names for them, one being the "Sala-abajou mife", meaning "the foreign place" referring to an area with some recently built homes that housed the foreigners. The area was also heavily guarded, and the locals were prohibited from going close to the region.

They had their land taken from them, given to foreigners, and then were banned from getting close to it in the first place by their own government.

I felt a crack in my voice when I explained this section to Esi. My inward anger at this realization had woven into the sounds of my voice and its weight caused me to pause.

I looked at Esi's unbroken expressions. Her eyes were full of keen interest about the direction I was leading her to. The story had hooked her the same way it hooked me.

I continued.

The discoveries I had made painted a daunting picture. I had found puzzle pieces that seemed to connect and fit together but the whole puzzle still didn't fully make sense. I knew of the outcome being the anomaly, though my discoveries still didn't have any direct connections to it. If this were a court case, it would be dismissed for lack of correlated evidence.

If I could prove that the anomaly started from Gbilepa, then this would make a case, but I couldn't.

Even after I sorted the posts in order of who posted earliest, I couldn't prove that the locations of all those who posted about the anomaly at the beginning, were in a radius close to Gbilepa. Most of the accounts didn't have their locations posted, and of the ones with their locations, none were from Gbilepa and only a few were even mildly close in range. It could be argued that the ones closest may have died first, but everything would just be speculation at that point.

However, if I could prove that the scientists were working on something directly connected to the anomaly, then I could make a sound case.

So, I asked myself what kind of research were they doing to cause this? I had found most of the other scientists as easily as I had found Mathéo. Their domains were in fields that either centered or complimented molecular biology. Was this outcome an accident or done with intention? And why did France go through the trouble of setting up a site here rather than their own country?

They clearly either expected a situation like this or were fully aware of the risks; what other reason could there be?

I spent the last hour and half of my search looking into their research for anything that might add more depth into what they were working on. I even paid to get past the paywall.

I had most of their names, so finding their prior research was easy. The research I found was intriguing but the only paper that had any mention of botany was a research paper on synthetic biology in November of 2013 which involved five of the scientists in the group.

The paper titled "*Biology merges Biology: What could be learned from plant biology to improve human biology.*"

The research paper talks about the different ways we could learn from plant engineering and mutations to improve human biology. It speaks of benefits like curing multiple diseases, developing the ability of body regeneration, better adaptation abilities, as well as general improvement of human genetics and more by learning to incorporate all the good parts about plant biology into human biology. I couldn't understand all the equations and elements it talked about on a deeper level but that was the entire premise — a merging of two.

The paper wasn't received exceptionally well, and people had a lot of comments on the website of how infeasible the idea was. The scientists argued that it would take more research to break the discoveries but the science was still a possibility under the right circumstances.

This finding made the most sense about what they were working on. What do those blue things coming out of the ground look like to you? Don't they look like large mutated plants?

Whatever they did there must have gone wrong; that is the only logical explanation for this. They caused this.

My voice cracked again.

Esi stared at me more intently than she ever had before. Her mouth hadn't spoken but her eyes told me what she was thinking before she even said a word. "*We have to tell the world. We are printing this tonight for tomorrow's paper.*" She said in a straight tone of conviction.

"*Tonight?*" I asked.

I had the connecting pieces for a story but tonight seemed too sudden. I would normally need to interview sources and triple check my facts, though in this case, I had no human sources to corroborate with.

The evidence looked convincing to both of us, but would it look the same to the world?

"*Yes. People need to know who is responsible for all that loss. Who was responsible for all those lives, they need justice!*"

I saw the rage in her eyes while she spoke, and I had no response to her words. She was right; people needed to know.

I looked at the time and it was just two minutes shy of 10:40pm. We had just a little over an hour to make an article for the front page and send the update.

The next hour that passed was surreal to say the least. It felt like an out-of-body experience where I had to relive my past experiences through someone else's eyes. Though Esi's eyes had a sharpness to them, like I was looking through an ultra-focused lens. We combed over the evidence, saving screenshots and videos from all the sources we had. We unspooled the giant web of threads together, drawing a clear outline for all to see.

"*What do you want to call it?*" Esi asked.

I didn't know. This was my biggest story ever and I had no name for it. I never imagined there was a story like this to find even when I started to search. Now that I had it, my mind went blank.

"*The sins of a monster.*" I said, as it finally came to me, clear and concise.

Yes, that was it; that was the name to use.

When the article finished, I stared at the black and white on the screen as if they were speaking to me. Was this the objective truth? It had to be, right? Everything made sense, it did. My intuition wouldn't lead me wrong.

I am the finder of truth, and I have found the ultimate story.

I clicked the button to forward the updates to the printing company, and Esi called to confirm it had arrived.

Ten minutes later, the watch struck midnight signaling the countdown toward the revelation.

I felt a heaviness in the depths of my heart. Is this anxiety? As a journalist, you put your work into the world and have no idea how it would be interpreted. Would it be widely accepted or criticized? Would people see the truth just like I have, or claim it is false?

I guess it doesn't matter now; I have done what was destined. Whatever happens from now will be for the world to decide.

"There is no greater gift you can give or receive than to honor your calling. It's why you were born. And how you become most truly alive." Oprah Winfrey.

About the author

Kiki Yaw Sarpong is a Boston based fiction novelist. He was born in Accra, Ghana, moved to America as a young college student. He pursued a Bachelor of Science degree in Mechatronics Engineering at Pennsylvania Western

University, and continued to pursue a Master's in Robotics at New York University. Presently, Kiki works as an Engineer and Novelist. Kiki has always had a deep passion and appreciation for storytelling, his favorites being mostly inclined toward Sci-fi and Fantasy. In Kiki's free time, he likes to watch long video essays about beloved movies and tv shows, or go biking through beautiful scenery.

Follow my socials:

https://linktr.ee/kikisarpong

Also by

www.ingramcontent.com/pod-product-compliance
Lightning Source LLC
Chambersburg PA
CBHW020313150626
46552CB00022B/2871